WHO'S COUNTING?

NANCY TAFURI

GREENWILLOW BOOKS · NEW YORK

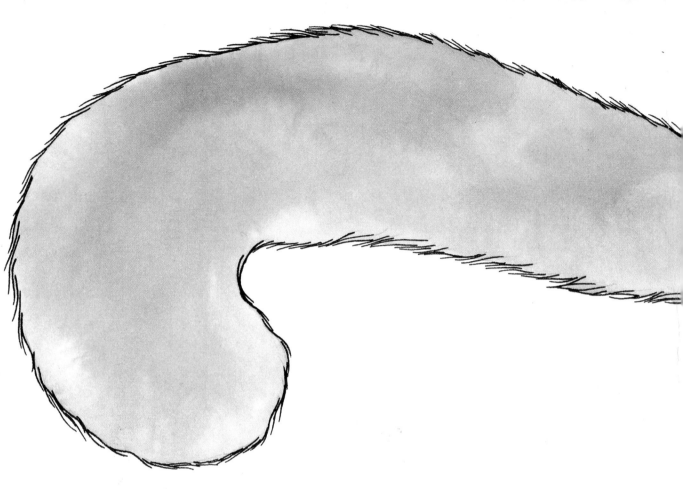

FOR ADA

A black line was combined with watercolor
paints for the full-color illustrations.
The text type is ITC Weiderman.

Printed in Hong Kong by South China Printing Co.
First Edition   10 9 8 7 6 5 4 3 2 1

Library of Congress Cataloging-in-Publication Data
Tafuri, Nancy.   Who's counting?
Summary: Text and illustrations of a variety of
animals introduce the numbers one through ten.
1. Counting—Juvenile literature.
[1. Counting]   I. Title.
QA113.T34 1986   513′.2 [E]   85-17702
ISBN 0-688-06130-3
ISBN 0-688-06131-1 (lib. bdg.)

1 SQUIRREL

2 BIRDS

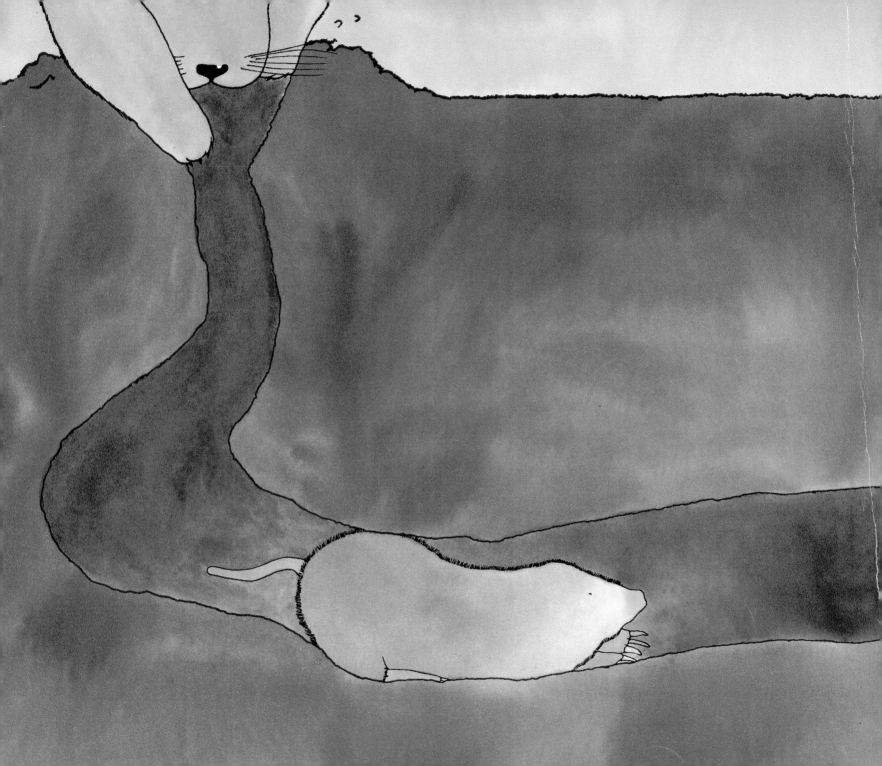

3 MOLES

4 GEESE

5

EGGS

6 PIGLETS

7 RABBITS

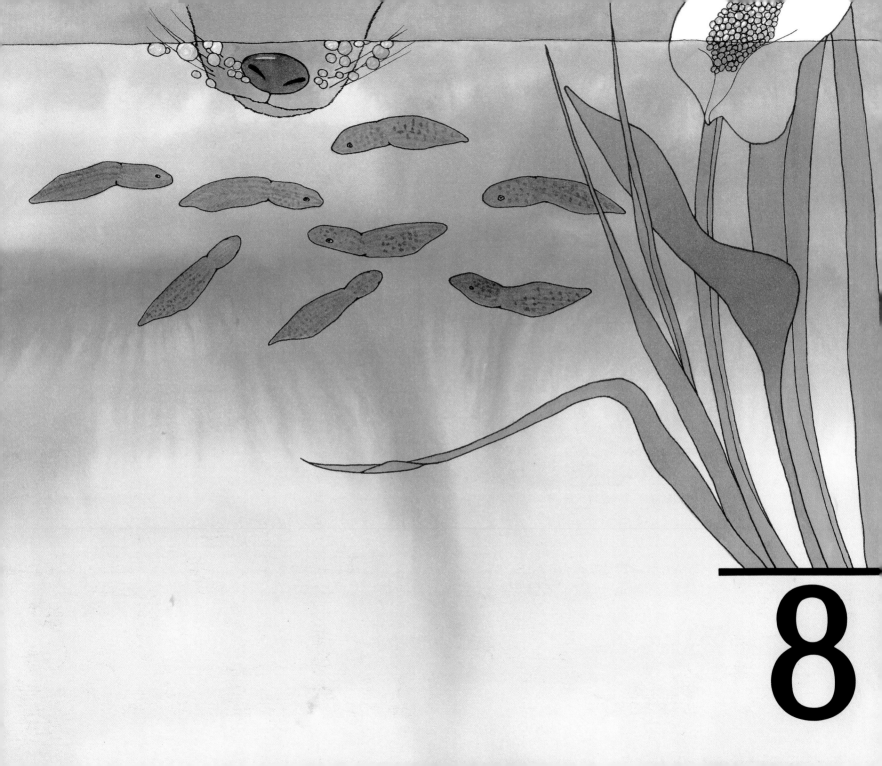

8

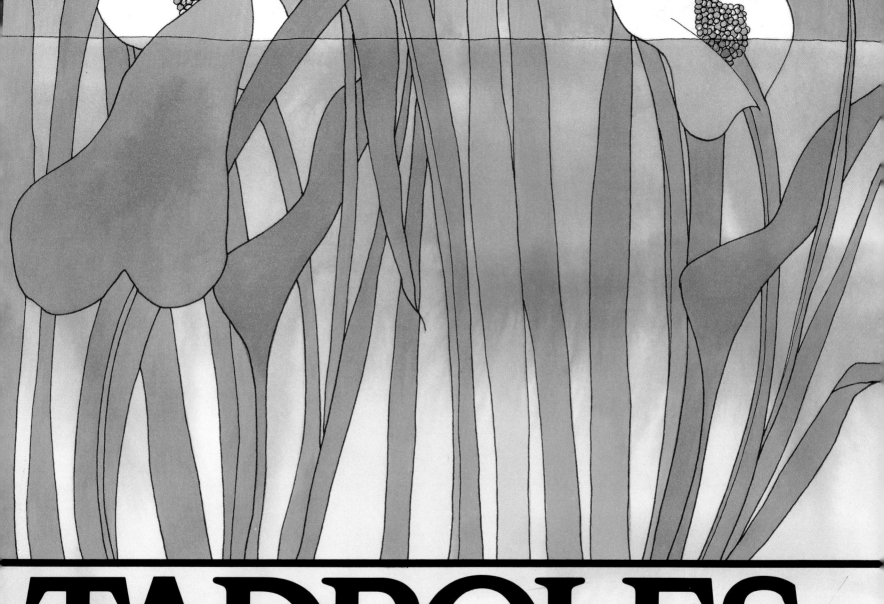

TADPOLES

9 FLOWERS

AND

10 PUPPIES-

EATING!